DARK LIGHT

PORTALS OF TRANSFORMATION

By

Ernest Antwi

Copyright © 2020 by Ernest Antwi

Cover and art design
by
WMW LLC

"But by the grace of God I am what I am…"
1 Corinthians 15:10

I dedicate this book to my earthly father, Dr. Ernest Kofi Antwi, my mother, Salomey Nsowah, and my sister, Nana Antwi. I want to thank my friends, Vanessa Hertweck and Luisa Condorelli, for being wonderful muses; I thank you both for your inspiration, adversarial tactics, friendship, and for igniting erotic desires in my soul.

I also want to thank my enemies for making me wiser, helping me to mature, and empowering me through affliction and ruthless lessons. Thank you, Father, for initiating me into the dark night of the soul because it opened my mind to otherworldly dimensions and increased my power and wisdom.

Thank you, Luisa, for teaching me that my darkness is a part of me but does not automatically define who I am as a person.

Above all else, I thank my Heavenly Father and the universe for sustaining me through pain and pleasure. I thank the universe for uplifting my soul through many lessons from many different people and situations. Heavenly Father and Universe, I thank and bless you.

Amen.

Table of Contents

DARK LIGHT

PORTALS OF TRANSFORMATION

Transform My Life

Heavenly Father, take me into the wilderness of your Word!
Take my soul out of the brewing sickness of worldly pleasures!
Wake my soul to the richness of your Word!
Free me from foolish passivity!
Free me from timidness!
Free me from limpness!
Quicken my soul with the Lion of Judah!
Lord God, electrify my soul with your might!
Guide me to the wealth of God's Word!
Crown me with wisdom!
With your Word, elevate my soul with gold, silver, and rubies!
Imbue my soul with your Word's marvelous power!

Shaped Unto Rejection and Rebellion

A dark, black shroud engulfs my life.
Confusion is my close companion.
Self-pity is my intimate lover.
Rebellion, a friend closer than a brother.
My family and I war against the divine.
Lusty perversion is my mother.
Poisonous seduction is my father.
My inheritance, the double-minded spirit.
I have become a prince of despair.
Look into my eyes and witness oblivion.
I speak, but the only sound is noisy, screeching
static.
The Father has turned his back on me,
So I have turned my back on the Father.

Ernest Antwi

Vanessa's Rapture by the Brown Lord

Under the cloak of night, the Brown Lord enters
Vanessa's sweetly-scented night chamber.
He tightly binds her arms and legs into an erotic sex
package.
He gags her with his golden, psychic lasso.
He ignites her body like a match with a tug of his
golden lasso.
She is gagged and blushed, his drooling sex slave.
Her sexy, red plum ass jiggles as he slaps it.
With strong, muscular arms, he turns her over;
Her sultry flesh jumps!
Telepathically, he exclaims, "Stop fighting and enjoy
what I have to offer."
Fiery eyes gaze into her soul.
Sharp pain penetrates her body as he serves her a
hard thing.
She surrenders as he turns her mind into a seething
cauldron of pleasure.
His power causes her muscles to jump and quiver.
Primal needs and urges brim, then overflow.
Ecstasy abounds with his thumb in her bum.
He growls as he pushes his hard thing into her
joyous love hole,
Sending lightning bolts of pleasure throughout her
body.
Her face twists with desire and upturns in rapture.
Magic hands meld bliss and pain.

He growls, she shrieks.
His strong hands around her red blush throat dare her to come and dare her not to.
He manhandles her sex, pounding her meat like a well-trained chef.
She squirts and gushes, her eyes rolling back in ecstasy.
His salty seed and her sweet nectar combine.
Her moans of pleading, whimpering, and begging fill the cosmos and displace the astral stars. [1]
He decorates her body with teeth marks, bruises, and welts of ecstasy.
In her psyche, he has marked his territory.

Footnote: Vanessa means colorful butterfly; she is my power animal that came to me in the flesh to touch my heart and help me along with my metamorphous.

---

[1]Astral World – An imagined world that parallels with the physical dimension that is treated as reality, while charged with emotion and intent.

Artifice of Rejection

She captures my eyes with her seductive beauty.
She tantalizes my soul with promises of warmth.
With an iced heart, she rejects me as quickly as she
pulled me in,
Filling my soul with the cold venom of inadequacy.
She baits me in with her perky, full breasts, lavish
thighs, and firm, plump ass,
Only to leave me desolate with rejection.
She rejects me, leaves me wanting more.
She toys with me as a house feline toys with its
found prey.
My senses betray me as she degrades my soul with
her artifice.
She won't let me into the beauty of her physical
chambers,
Yet like a succubus, drains me with her astral
debaucheries.
Her artifice creates an earthquake of frustration in
my soul.
I am crushed with wild frustrations under the rubble
of rejection.
Crushed and defeated,
I still desire her, like a crazed fool.

Erotic Milkshake Poem

In the arms of my love, Vanessa:
She fills my mouth with her sweet, fleshy
strawberry.
Her lips are sweet, divine, and juicy with erotic love.
With his fingertips, he feeds her sweet banana;
Sweet and firm, the way she likes it.
Her natural scent fills his nostrils with heady desire.
She inhales the divine scent of cum;
She oozes strawberry nectar from her canal of love.
Her desirous, plump ass cheeks are in his hands;
She is in his grasp, and desire swallows them.
A fire grows within his muscular belly.
His manhood fills with the incarnate fire of Chango.
Aggression twists his face, and he envelops her.
Her hair and neck smell ripe for the picking.
He licks her from her sultry neck to her pink,
delectable nipples.
She is his living treat; he turns her into an erotic
milkshake.
He kisses her lovingly on the forehead,
while she pulls his tan banana out of his boxers.
He gets harder than Italian oak as she strokes his
chub;
Throbbing, aching needs build.
He is her joy of joys; she is his mighty strength.
She jumps up and wraps her lavish thighs around
him.

He pounds her wet, sopping quim, while grabbing her ass tightly.
He shakes her soul to an erotic oblivion; their eyes roll back into a divine rapture.
They get lost in the vibrations of their erotic dance.
Steamy sweat glistens; the heat of love emanates from their bodies.
He decorates her with the royal pearls of Poseidon.
By the power of the Sea God, he makes a beautiful mess of her.
Her long, black luminous hair is filled with glistening love pearls.

Erotic and Sensual Connect with Vanessa

I gaze upon Vanessa with my astral eyes.
I feel her heart beat across the distance of the
quantum jump.[2]
I desire her as I gaze upon her beauty from afar.
In the ecstasy of my desire, I invoke the Haitian gate
opener, Papa Legba.
I compel her to connect with me.

Let our eyes connect.
Let our energy intertwine, becoming a twin flame.
Let us talk of our days of innocence.
My face becomes twisted with lust.
Pain sets in from my throbbing love tool;
I need her to relieve me.
I grab her, with intent to ravage her.
I pull her long, black hair, drawing her head back.
I teleport her to a tantric oasis.

My mind gets lost in the Scent of her wondrous
flesh.
I suck her neck like a baby chimp sucks the sweet
juices from a fleshy mango fruit
And grab her wet portal of love like a crazed man
who just found gold.
She is wearing tight baby blue volleyball shorts.

---

[2] Across the Quantum – A belief exerted by the author that consciousness
is like a plain of various energy levels.

They are soaked with desire and anticipation.
My thumb between the slit of her inner left thigh,
I yank her shorts off and use them to cuff her legs
together.

Like a Siberian husky coming home,
I slide my head through her lavish thighs.
Like a rock bass in the Erie Canal,
I dip myself in her golden lake;
My tongue partakes of her sopping wet quim.
Her moans travel as a ripple through the quantum
sea.
I feel like a captain of a living sea ship.
We travel at quantum speed throughout the
psychedelic cosmos as we climax.

My mouth fills with her divine nectar.
My nose quivers from the joy of being enveloped in
her sweet scent.
Her pleasure becomes my pleasure as we melt into
one being.
We flow into one another as the Niagara River falls
into itself.
Our egos dissolve into one as we ascend to Olympus,
Like the steamy mist from Victoria Falls.
We explode like a Supernova before the assembly of
the gods.
We are reborn apart in the earthly, but forever
cosmically connected.

The Sleeper Has Awakened

Heavenly Father, keep me steady with wisdom!
Mighty Chango, infuse me with your blood!
Increase my testosterone!
Help me find my soul!
Fill my heart with your jet fuel!
Propel me out of this emotional purgatory!

Free me from past trauma.
Insert the hammer into the cosmos,
Drawing fire and power and the desire to win.
Endow my soul with power,
Wake me from the zombie trance,
Pull me out of the quicksand of self-pity.
Illuminate my eyes with your electrifying passion.

Behold, the sleeper has awakened!
A son of Chango, I am.
I walk in life with purpose.
Chango adorns my neck with power,
A red necklace of ambition.
The Prison of Fear gives way to the Freedom of
Courage.
I am a calculated risk-taker.
I am a winner.
I am a lover of life.

Chango endows me with the warrior Hawk spirit.

I am relentless in the pursuit of my goals.
Chango is in my blood, so I soar high.
Wisdom is in my mind, so I fly unhindered.
With God's Word in my mind, I fly by divine
purpose.

Hope for Better

No friends.
Stuck in the stupor of the past,
Lost.
My purpose eludes me.
I am in search.
Praying for courage and strength,
Longing for something better.
It is darkest just before the dawn.

Vanessa Hertweck: My Muse

Her long, golden-blonde hair majestically flows and
adorns the sides of her angelic face.
It is oval-shaped with delectable and sharp
cheekbones.
Her bright, goofy smile, intoxicating laugh, and
Joyous spirit uplifts me like the laughing Buddha;
I love her spunky and fun personality.
Her mascara outlines her deep and luring hazel-
brown eyes.
I find her eyes entrancing; they make me drunk with
erotic desire.
Her seductive eyes fall under arched, yet unruly
eyebrows.
Her cute, Roman nose accents her thin, peach-
colored lips.
Her lightly-freckled skin is smooth, kissed with an
even, golden tan by Apollo.
I find her stature full of poise and grace.
Her body is petite and statuesque;
Her hands are delicate, yet strong at her side, along
her firm thighs.
I have found my sweet muse.

Intentional Living

Intention.
Double-Edged Sword of Intention,
Reap what I sow:
Power and Warning intertwined.
Transform my world intentionally.
With each stroke of my pen, I conjure up a new reality.
I conjure a reality that exudes God's purpose.
I give birth to myself.
I am success as I live it.

Ernest Antwi

The Hermit's Cocoon

The wrong people are around me.
Friends. Enemies. Acquaintances. Strangers.
People with evil intentions
Dry me up.
They dry up my bones.
I grow old before my time,
I find refuge in solitude.
One comfort gives me hope:
The sacred texts of God's Word.
I am a hermit,
I lock myself away,
I am in mediation,
Locked away tightly in God's Word.
I am a filthy maggot in a Holy Cocoon.
God whispers to my torn soul,
And I hear, "Be ye transformed!"
I am imbued with splendor,
My soul is transformed:
Filthy maggot to majestic butterfly.
Discernment is my right wing,
Proper timing is my left.
I soar high above my enemies;
I am high but among them, with feet firmly planted.
I am in the world, but not of it.

Luciferian Desires for Vanessa Hertweck

In the present, looking in the mirror of the past, I
could have had Vanessa.]
Even only for one passionate night, I could have had
her.
I was too nice. I wasn't assertive enough. I wasn't
man enough.
Looking in the mirror of the present, I still want her.
I am still captivated by her eyes.
I desire her intensely and am willing to do anything.
I'm willing to pay the price to be with her and feel
her sultry heat.
I am willing to invoke that demon to ignite her lust
to my desire.
My desire is to ravage her from a full moon night
until the dawn of day.
I say, by Lucifer, I don't care;
I pick her off as fruit from a forbidden holly tree.
My lust is ignited. I compel her soul to come to me; I
captivate her.
I charm her with these purple, satin sheets;M She is
mine tonight.
I embrace her in a delicious, breathtaking French
kiss.
I pull her silky, black hair back.
I grab and squeeze her breast, putting it into my
mouth.
I throw her on the bed.

She is engulfed in the silky bed sheets.
She is my prisoner, spellbound by my lust and pleasure. Vanessa moans in ecstasy.
"Oh Vanessa, your moan is music to my ears," I whisper.
I partake of Vanessa's cunt as honey-covered cannoli.
Intense, lusty pleasure grips her.
I take her senses to a delectable pain as I invade her tight asshole.
Like that devil, Eros, I erotically lick her heart-shaped ass.
I turn her sexy body around and bury her head in cinnamon-perfumed sheets.
Her soft, heart-shaped, sugary ass in the air,
I slap her ass; the slap sounds Zeus's thunder.
Her body is taken hostage with the electrifying thrill of passion and the fiery lust of Eros.
With her moans, she sings a lustful song that she desires more.
With a devil's tongue, I cool her red, plum ass by licking her
From her sugary cunt to her tight asshole.
Her body responds like a husky pup being licked by its mother.
Her eyes roll back into her eyelids in pleasure.
Pleasure and pain combine to produce unearthly, mind-blowing orgasms.
For a split second, she loses her mind as she

ejaculates,
While simultaneously defecating on herself.
She loses herself, but I bring her back to me with the
kiss of Zeus on the forehead.
This night she won't remember; at the same time,
she will never forget!
I throw her spirit back to that insipid hunk of flesh
she calls a husband.

Ernest Antwi

My Father: A Fine Teacher

My father, a fine teacher.
His lessons were as pain and fire.
He ignited my soul to self-destruction.
In smokeless fire, I learned not to compromise my
soul.

For good or evil, he is my father.
In righteousness and wickedness, he was my best
teacher.
With cruel ruthlessness, he seared his teachings into
my soul.
He taught me the nefarious horrors of this life.
He taught me the power of confusion and deception.

Like Lucifer, he taught me to despise the external
savior.
When he stole my beloved, Mother Mnemosyne, he
taught me loss.
He taught me the dark truth of human nature.
I learned that people will always try to hurt you.

My father's light was the fire of painful experiences.
I learned that pain is a fine teacher.
In the classroom of suffering, I learned treachery.
In the seat of discomfort,
I experienced the misery of loneliness.

Like Lucifer and Coeus,
He taught me that self-belief[3] is the highest virtue.
In pain, he woke me up from dependence to others'
words.
As he seared my soul,
I found my voice in a scream.
He was the catalyst of my rebirth.
I died as his son,
I was reborn as a powerless witch.

With my father, I learned not to reason with
madness.
Just as he destroyed, I could create.
In hope and love, I create a new self.
With reason and logic, I give birth to a better me.
I arise from the ashes of his teachings.
I inhale the revitalizing air of self-belief and self-
determination;
My eyes shine bright with confidence.

---

[3] Self-Belief – Confidence in one's abilities, thoughts, and will to succeed
in any and all endeavors.

Vanessa Hertweck: My Virgin Flower

The Eternal God tips His ruby chalice and pours out
his Holy Spirit on you. It falls as a majestic waterfall
and showers you with loving rebirth.

You become a dying star in the midnight sky, the
emergence of a breathtaking supernova; then you
emerge whole in righteousness.

Your chastity flourishes, and you arise as a supple
virgin, whose flower is pure in a fountain of
sparkling water.

You are pure like a white lotus flower of the valley.
You are a lotus and the blooming of purity. Pure is
your wonderful flower, blooming and releasing the
sweet fragrance of God's breath.

Your flesh is as a virgin field, emanating purity and
the potential for great riches.

The after-shower scent of your body takes my mind
to the height of the seven wonders of the world, all at
once. My soul becomes crazed in the ecstasy of the
experience; I become a bottle of champagne being
poured all over your nude body, splashing with joy.

Your blonde hair holds strands of beauty, and its

dark transitions reflect the royalty of an African hawk. You have the intuition of a princess of Ancient Babylon; your lovely hair reflects your quick insight and is a gift from God.

Your loving face is the soaring of a dove. Your face is peaceful, and even when you become mad, your eyes are as precious rubies to me.

I love your tasty personality, and your conversation is an earthly symphony to my ears; you pull me into your world with your instruments of divinity, your lips, and the erotic melodies of your tongue; your words are as colorful butterflies in my mind, reflecting the beautiful light of the sun.

You are wonderful, like a French bouquet of roses. Your heart is a mysterious red rose, and God drops himself on you as a ball of fire. Your heart flames and your rose blossoms as it burns without burning, then it becomes incense, hurling and swirling with fiery smoke, releasing the sweetest fragrance.

At the Altar of Venus with Vanessa

I am
Embracing, caressing, and kissing
My love,
My dove,
My Vanessa.
Passionately, tenderly, and sweetly,
Riding into the awe of rapture,
At the altar of Venus.

Vanessa Hertweck: Alluring and Seductive

V – Virtuous devil with the voice of a seraph,
A – Alluring, sugary, golden honeycomb,
N – Naughty and deliciously dangerous succubus.
E – Elegant and enchanting goddess, like Aphrodite,
S – Seductive bag full of naughty little tricks.
S – Sexy scent from vanilla-bean Colombian coffee,
A – Adored and favored by the gods of paradise.

H – Hot and spicy lemon-drop, pepper, and
cinnamon whiskey,
E – Elegant sway of tantalizing hips,
R – Radiant sun-kissed sapphire,
T – Tasty and pleasantly-sweet honeycomb from
heaven,
W – Wild and cunning red Sicilian fox,
E – Exceptionally witty and bright, alluring goddess,
like Aurora,
C – Charming, colorful melody of an enchanted
Brazilian forest,
K – Kinky and fun like Aphrodite and forever
leaving me wanting more.

Vanessa Hertweck: A Sweet, but Treacherous Garden

Your hair is lovely like a foxtail, a gift from God. You excite me like good herb.

You are the light in my eye, a beautiful firework show in the midnight sky.

Your small, petite shape is sexy. You are attractive like an angel of heaven.

Your lies and deceptions are a storm in my mind. I get caught up in your whirlwind. But God is my Buckler and my Rock. I find a stable place in Him.

You are my Garden of Eden, and sweet are your grapes from the vine. Your fine wine is mixed with marijuana, and your romantic juice is intoxicating.

The sweet fragrance of your wine is the aroma of something better in my life; the bubbles in my wine glass take me to a joyous dimension.

You are a gift from God, and sensual is your Garden. You are my majestic Eve.

Your tasty kiss is the breath of God, the spark at creation, and the manifestation of Eden.

A black hole is your love, deep and mysterious. The dew of your garden is heavy and strong; it jets me to an erotic new dimension.

Cold and evil is your heart. I get lost in your deceptions. You bring me to destruction; only God can save me. I still want more.

I pour dark red wine on your chest; it runs down your loveliness, and I drink from between your legs.

The flesh between your legs is the honey bread of death. I eat my fill and wash it down with your wine of illusions; my eyes roll back in pain and joy, swirling in ecstasy.

I get lost in your trance; in your eyes, I go to the dark side of the moon and come back a new man.

I put my mouth to your small, wonderful melon. I partake of its mango's nectar; it is my strength. My blood becomes a boiling fire.

Your thighs are like warm bread on my rib cage.
Toasty is your love.

When we come together, it is fire and ice. We
threaten each other with sweet death. I lick your
neck with spice and herb; behind your ear is
honeycomb.

I thrust my hips into your sweet death. I am turned
on by your sugary challenge; I may lose my life in
your death-trap.

Like a mighty warrior and a foolish boy, I proceed
forward in your treacherous Garden. Sweet is your
fruit, and ominous is your warmth.

Your icy warmth is painful, but I want more. Please
let me have more, my Sweet Vanessa.

Arrival of Death

I wish death upon you.
When your psychic force fields give way to a
consuming terror,
Then you will know Death has arrived.
When your life has crumbled before your eyes,
You will know Death has arrived.
When an ice-cold paralyzes, overtakes your body
and soul,
Then you will know the Angel of Death is upon you.
Overshadowed by darkness,
Your body will lie still and lifeless,
Your body, emitting the awful stench of Death's
perfume.
Your body, overtaken by maggots,
And the earth swallowing you up into its belly:
I wish death upon you.

Ernest Antwi

A La Playa con Mi Amor

In a carnal dream of delight,
I'm wrapped in the fine linen of a starry midnight
sky.
On the Persian carpet of mysteries,
I lay with my love, Vanessa.
En La Playa de Carmen,
We soak in one another's erotic seduction.

I gaze on her beauty with wondrous delight.
Her delicious feminine form is adorned with a sexy
Venus sky blue bikini.
Like a heady young boy, I unpack her like a
Christmas gift.
I slowly open the chambers of Olympus, making my
way to her love.

At her altar, I make libation with coconut oil.
I tease her by running my hands over her
womanhood.
With my mouth, I partake of her ambrosia.
I empower her to express her pleasure.
In worship, we give offerings of ecstasy to the gods.

Awe of Vanessa

Vanessa:
She is divine and full of beauty.
Her wondrous countenance glows like moonlight,
Her supple skin a mix of milk and Caramel.
Her hair is the roots and strength of an Ethiopian
Coral tree.
Her eyes reveal perfect wisdom.
She is excellent and full of delight:
Vanessa.

Consumed by the Queen Black Widow

Her mouth is a palace of ruin.
Her tongue is Satan enthroned.
Her teeth are sparkling rubies, reflecting deception.

She is as beautiful as she is treacherous.
When she speaks, she spins wickedness.
Only a few have seen her true form.

Her Kingdom is the web of the black widow spider.
At the center, she scatters the skulls of wise men.
Her scepter is the femur of a powerful Zulu warrior.

Her royal pearl crown is made from stolen gold and
silver.
Her lavish necklace is made from the testicles of
princes.
She enchants, traps, and devours the innocent.

When I came to her, I came as a humble sage.
In her eyes, I was a delicious prospect.
I was a tasty insect to be devoured.

She promised to open my spiritual eyes with her
mysteries.
She revealed her secrets, only to reveal my
foolishness
And the brilliance of her treachery.

I became her damn fool and plaything.
She left lesions on my soul.
With dishonor, she wrapped me up in her cocoon of
destruction.

When I emerged, I was a mystic butterfly with
broken wings,
Colored in shame.
In the end, my mind was gone from me: I was left in
a dismal state.

Ernest Antwi

Deliver Me from the Scarlet Witch

I am a slave.
I ask Father God, "Free my soul?"
I have fallen and found myself in the cruel snare of a
scarlet witch.
Her mouth is a bottomless pit, full of venomous
vipers.
My wounds are deep and severe; my soul is being
overtaken by her poison.
My soul is wounded; I need a holy redeemer.
Lord God, please forgive me for my folly.
I believed the lie and artifice of a scarlet witch over
your Words.
Every night, she attempts to drag my soul down to
hell.
My redeemer delivers my soul from the deadly cords
of sin.
Because of her, my enemies are in search of me like
hungry wolves.
Let me be enveloped in sage smoke and hidden from
her bloodthirsty eyes!
In the spring well by the river of purification, I wash
myself.
With the scissors of truth, I groom myself to
righteousness.
My redeemer takes my guilt and shame away.
Ignite my soul to confidence!

Destruction and Death

Smoldering anger ravages my soul;
The windows of my soul are blacked out,
Lesions fill my body.
The story of me is a sad one.
The sweet lady death is not far.

Finding Love Poem

Ernest and Vanessa, Twin-flamed lovers.
She quickens his soul with loyalty.
He has found his soulmate.
She is his supple nymph.
His soul is hydrated by her joyous love.
Her skin is sun-kissed to an olive tone.
He gazes into her deep, brown eyes, and his face
brightens with joy.
She is an Archer of Love.
He is smitten with her intoxicating personality.
She has made him drunk with fiery love.
His stony heart has melted away with her warm, soft
gaze.
She shot her arrow of love through the fortress of his
heart.
His soul is seized, ignited with joy.
Her youthful flame chases away the darkness from
his soul.
He has found his Latin American queen.
She is smitten by his gravitas and passion for her.
She has found her mighty protector and dark king.
They become one in their psychic cocoon of love.

Give Birth to Your Christ

She becomes one with her God force.
She breathes in the might of the Spirit.
She becomes pregnant with divine light.
Her third eye awakens to truth.
She possesses the keys to freedom.
Power and truth flow through her belly.
A Lioness of the cosmos,
Her head is elevated to righteousness.
By the Spirit,
Her tongue is tamed with "Right Speech."
Like a good teacher,
She uplifts the downtrodden souls of the wayward.
With healing heart energy,
She empowers the wayward to walk out of a maze of
confusion.
She quickens the souls of both foe and friend.
The lamp of their soul becomes bright with
confidence.
She is the bride of salvation and righteousness.
In perfect love and trust,
As the Dove,
She ascends into the sky of joyful peace.

Henceforth: Chango!

Awaken the ghost in my brain,
Put to rest the spirit of fear!
That which is dead animates with life.
I resurrect like a Christ.

The Earth shakes and rumbles to reveal greatness:
A rose springs forth from limestone,
The baby blue sky gives birth to the sun.
The mighty Oak Tree remains still in a strong wind
of opposition.

The sky shifts into the might of Leo,
The sky roars with thunder and shoots lightning from
fierce eyes.
The alpha waves of a new beginning renew the face
of the mountain.
The eternal flame lights the womb of the cave.

The might of the Ethiopian drum is in line with
Earth's rhythm.
Mighty Chango steps forth out of the cave of
mysteries.
His muscular form is smokeless fire.
He is my elected commander-in-chief.
I salute you, Chango.

His Longing for Vanessa

Vanessa, his love—
He misses her with all his heart.
He desires her more than life itself.
He refuses to suffer the distance between them.
In haste,
He decides to have her by the power of Chango.
Under the soft glow of moonlight,
He invokes the powers of Chango.
Shimmering and smokeless fire shrouds his astral
form.
Across time and space,
He outwits the wild ape of the mind.
Like a strong wind, filled with the scent of myrrh,
He boldly enters her sacred sleeping chambers.
Her lovely female scent graces his astral nostrils.
His astral senses are enlivened with heady passions.
He gazes at her with his fiery eyes of desire.
Her body is as a temple of Venus.
He strums her violin at the altar.
She makes sweet musical moans of ecstasy.
With her sultry flesh, he has his fill.
They melt together in love.
With longing and passion,
They become lost in the sea of consciousness.
They find themselves in the reflection of one
another's souls.

I Am a Master

Self-pity is no more:
I am a master.
Self-indulgence is no more:
I am a master.
Self-loathing is no more:
I am a master.
I inhale three deep and refreshing breaths:
Light enters my soul.
I find myself in an eerie cemetery,
Under the glow of a full moon.
I am confronted by three nefarious demons.
I dodge the poisonous darts of self-pity with
compassion.
I parry the steely knives of self-loathing with
wisdom.
I intercept the tantalizing artifice of self-indulgence
with discipline.
I strike a death blow to the heart of self-pity.
I strangle the neck of self-indulgence.
I crush the head of self-loathing.
I bury my demons deep within the Earth.
I pray to Mother Goddess to swallow them into
oblivion:
Like the sun, I arise.
I am a transformed man:
My face is bright with confidence.

Majestic Web of Deception

As an eager and lost hermit,
I traveled through the might of air and sea.
Like an insect, I found myself trapped in the web of
life.
I was trapped but not without divine purpose.
I was in God's righteous web of power,
Each strand vibrating his Word of righteousness and
salvation for the human soul.
Each strand a lesson of pain and suffering,
Promising to bring me closer to my royal destiny.
As I gaze at the center of the web,
I see a primordial, formless void.
As I approach the center,
I am met with the hindrance of a majestic entity.

Her name was Luisa, the deceitful spider:
Her crafty web was a magical spell of deception.
She introduced herself as my savior.
She promised me reprieve from my suffering.
Her soft skin was fair, and her hair was velvet black.
Most of all, her words were charming and sweeter
than honey.

Looking back, God used her to break me down with
her wicked deceptions
Then empower me by drawing me closer to Him.
It was God who allowed her to have her way with

me.
She consumed me in the fire of her rage and pain.
She shackled my mind and made me her wretched
slave.
I became her laboring thief and her big, stupid fool.
She enveloped my mind in her cocoon of confusion
And left me in a dismal state of uncertainty.
To her delight, she fed off of my pain
And suffering as nourishing nectar.

She was clever and shrewd as she tried to steal my
hope and salvation.
Through her artifice, she taught me the importance
of self-honesty.
God used her to show me that salvation belongs to
Him alone.
Their lessons intertwined made a wiser and stronger
man.
Like a majestic dove, I spread my wings and took
flight,
Surrendering to the spirit of freedom and destiny.
With newfound eyes of vigilance,
I walk with divine purpose,
Fulfilling my divine destiny with every breath and
action.

Mental Transformation

I step out of my dismal state of mind.
With the holy silver cord of faith,
I free myself from the quicksand of destruction.
I tap into righteous thought and light my way to
success.
My mind is illuminated; I avoid the council of the
wicked.
I safely traverse amid the horrid scorpions of
deception.
I avoid the toxic spiders that weave traps.
I outwit the evil, red-eyed lizard of fear, who strives
to lead me astray.
I become the change I desire by filling my heart with
compassion.
My old mental wasteland gives way to fields of
prosperity.
I find myself surrounded by wonder and majesty.
The horrid scorpion gives way to the peaceful and
lovely dove.
The deceitful spider gives way to the noble and far-
seeing giraffe.
The scary, red-eyed lizard gives way to the wise and
powerful elephant.

Ernest and Vanessa: Our Relationship

Across time and space,
My parched soul thirsts for your soft touch.
With a deep sense of urgency,
I race into your arms to quench my dying soul.
I gaze into your deep, wondrous, hazel eyes, and my
soul is filled with the water of life.
Your gaze becomes trapped in mine.
Our eyes lock and ignite a luminous flame that
brightens the deepest darkness.
Your affection affects me, like a tranquilizing spring.
I feel at peace in your presence.
I grasp your soft and supple hands.
I gaze upon you, as you are my found treasure.
Our cocoon of love and intimacy transforms us.
We make plans for something beautiful.
We just met,
But we feel as if we've met before.
Despite the foreseeable challenges,
We find solace in our faith in one another.
We make a commitment to never surrender our love.
Let us eat, drink, explore, and talk.
Let us be merry in one another.

The Path to Inner Power

Heavenly Father, empower your son!
Grant me the electrifying power of Thor,
Grant me his Mighty Hammer and Strength.
Charge my right hand with power,
Ignite my heart to your healing Word.
I am filled with the power to remove obstacles with
creativity!
Tear down the bloodstained wall of my heart,
Bloodstained from the Trauma of abuse,
The words from an insecure father.
Help me to find that which was misplaced!
Help me to find my inner power!
Help me to find my heart!
Electrify my mind:
I am reborn,
My soul is found in you.

Finding My Power Through the Trials of Life

Lost in a sea of troubles,
Hindered by strong winds of setback,
Mind writhing with worry and anxiety:
The peace of something solid escapes me.

Thunderstorms threaten to steal my hope.
Hurricanes try to swallow me whole.
My mind submerged, but not drowned,
My power is reclaimed with the word, "NO!"

Resurrection is found through new perspectives on
God.
Seas of trouble become my precious stepping stones
to success,
Strong winds of setback come back to opportunity,
Imbued with my power as my soul resurrects.

Luisa: Queen of the Sicilian Witches

Luisa Condorelli
Rapacious monster, Magnetic black hole, Demonic
soothsayer,
Descendent of the sex demon Lilith and sister of the
Sicilian Medusa,
Who only cares about control, manipulation, and
domination,
Who feels that, "Might makes right,"
Who gives evil for good,
Who tried to destroy my soul with words of deceit,
Who tried to steal my spirit in a night of carnal
pleasure,
Who tried to kill me to hide our sin,
Who fears the truth, Christ, and righteousness,
Resident of Dante's second sphere of Hell:
Luisa Condorelli

Luisa Condorelli: Mi Santa de Muerte

When I first met her, our connection was as past life
lovers:
Her lovely face was the saving grace of Apollo.
She saved me from death and the horrors of night.
Her presence in my life was salvation and hope;
Her kindness was water to my thirst.

It was easy to love her.
She was my reprieve from my personal hell.
She was the soothing ointment for my wounds.
She was my saving angel of light,
A white dove to lift me from my dismal state.

It was nothing for me to share myself with her.
Willingly, I gave her the glistening pearls of my
soul.
Like a Venus flytrap, she turned against me.
For my pearls, she gave me her despiteful black coal.
For my love, she used me as a stupid donkey.
The illusions began sweeter than honeycomb nectar.
In the end, I was left with the bite of a viper.

The pleasant illusion was sweet no more.
The warm sun gave way to an entrapping moon.
Her light turned into a dark, ominous shroud.
Her wrath was a quiet thunderstorm in the distance.
Like a patient lioness in the Angolan marsh,

She is ready to overtake me with murderous
violence.
Her lovely flesh gave way to a pearl-white skeleton
of death.
She was an ugly mockery to life.

I moved, yet I was stuck.
With my own sin, she imprisoned me;
I was trapped on the boat of fools.
I was adrift down a gloomy Angkor Wat river to a
sorrowful end.
In my cold and unyielding shackles,
I groaned, "But things were so sweet…what
happened?"
She exhaled a cloud of French cigarette smoke.
Like a cruel woman of nobility,
She looked back at me with callous eyes, inflamed
with hate.
My stark and cold reality was that I was her woeful
slave.

Under the scarce-light moon,
I looked 'round about me to find no hope.
I'm left with the reality of my own foolishness.
The angry wolf howls treachery.
The hateful raven flaps its wings with deceit.
The nervous snake scurries away with fear.
The air is hard to breathe, filled with the pollution of
sin.

I felt so far from the God of truth.

My bones ached with guilt and sin.
I felt like I was losing my mind as life slowly left
me.
My end was nigh.
I screamed to God, "Where are you?"
I felt the mighty movement of the clouds
And heard the crackling of thunder.
God replied with the swiftness of lightning,
Asking me, "Where have you put me?"
I replied to him, "Forgive me and come back into my
life."

"Rise, my son!" he said.
His Words were like rejuvenating marrow to my
bones,
Strength to my soul,
And clarity to my mind.

Santa Muerte is no more as chaff in the whirlwind.
Away from the deception of Death,
Next to the power and truth of Christ,
I now stand.

Dark Mistress in My Soul

I take three deep, wondrous breaths and gaze inward.
I open my third eye to reveal the illuminous light of
my spirit.
My sight soars as high as the mighty eagle.
I see as deep and far as the wise and powerful owl.
I see the magical images of my dark, old soul.

I fly to the dark inner kingdom full of death, rebirth,
and desire.
I see the mistress of the shadows in the corner of my
soul.
She is like a thorny, black rose of death in my
psyche.
Her dark petals cast a shade of illuminous power.
At the center of my soul, the Dragon's blood incense
smolders and crackles at the altar.
The incense emits the scent of something powerful
to come.

I feel her presence as a brief, strong rush of warm
air.
My heart is filled with erotic desire and power.
Her tantalizing scent is that of a prostitute perfumed
with vanilla and cinnamon.
Her telepathic teachings are that of a high priestess.
Her seductive powers are from the dark side of the
moon.

Her lessons are filled with pain, then power.

Why do I love her?
Through her abuse, she taught me the type of woman to avoid.
Through her many slights, she taught me the importance of planning.
Through her spiteful behavior, she taught me to be cautious of everyone.
Through her sweet, but poisonous artifice, she taught me that salvation belongs to God alone.

Chango, Born Again!

With prophecy and wisdom,
His eyes become as bright as the midnight stars.

With the brilliance of his crown,
His soul is resurrected with might and confidence.

With his battle axe,
He is imbued with power and authority.

Through Chango,
He finds his inner strength.

He is adorned with royal red satin pants and a white
shirt of purification.[4]
He is Chango.

---

[4] The red represents virility, passion, and power, while the white
represents the justice of Chango.

Standing Firm Against Deception

In the presence of the fiery, red-eyed dragon of
destruction,
I choose to remain calm.
It subjects me to its demonic wiles.
It attempts to hypnotize me with seductive illusions.
I choose to remain centered in my faith.
With its deathly, hot breath,
It tries to intoxicate my mind with fear.
I choose to remain calm, cool, and confident.
In its rage, it engulfs me with fire.
I am consumed, but not burnt.
I stand at the gate of my mind,
Vigilantly guarding my heart against intrusion.
I never suffer my foot to be moved from the path of
righteousness.
I am firm in who I am, as I stand my ground against
the falsehoods of the dragon:
I stand against the illusions that threaten to blind me!
I stand against the lies that threaten to kill my soul!
I stand against the artifice that threatens to steal my
happiness!
I am unmoved in its terrible and fierce roar.
I find peace in my faith.
I tap into my inner truth.
I see a beautiful white dove as peace overtakes my
soul.

As I walk further down the path of righteousness,
The might and dragon fade away into nothingness.
I become peace and ascend out of the presence of
darkness.

Thunder and Wind for My Enemies

Thunder, Lightning, and then the Power:
I uplift my right arm, high into the sky.
I receive the power to eviscerate my enemies.
Filled with power, I shake the ground.
I cause my enemies to stumble and fall.
They choke on their evil schemes and gossip.
In fiery rage, they shoot poisonous darts of deception
at me.
I channel the wisdom within and gracefully disarm
them.
I cause the sky to roar with power like an African
lion.
With murderous anger, they fire darts of death at me.
I stir the wind and engulf them in their own
destruction.

Flowing Nowhere and Everywhere

Flowing, flowing as the shapeless substance: water.

I separate myself from my decaying form;

I must relinquish "self."

I'm flowing into the center of pure being,

A place and an entity: nowhere and everywhere.

Duality is no more.

Holy Edification Process

An isolated locality of choice, a place between nowhere and somewhere; a grand hall of salvation, where new beginnings and ruinous ends are thinly separated. I find myself in the all-consuming presence of the archangel Michael; I am sitting in a grand, wooden chair of timelessness. In a wondrous gaze, I view the stupendous profile of the majestic warrior; I am trapped in a paralyzing awe at how the Heavenly Father could create a being with such a superb and sophisticated martial poise. With vocal grandeur, Michael exclaims, "This is the day the Lord has made." I quickly bring my eyes forward in a deep, disciplined gaze and begin to look inward. Suddenly, I begin to sense a cleansing light with the splendor and power of a solar flare emanating from the angelic warrior's eyes. He envelops me in a fierce blaze of light; something in me screams out in evil anger as my soul is purged from demonic bondage and my dark side is balanced with the righteousness of God. The imperial light begins to personify a holy and majestic image of a lion that claws and tears away at the decaying image of my old self. I'm consumed in a quick pattern, a writhing tornado of light. With every evolution, I find myself endowed with the power and majesty of the holy warrior spirit: I embrace a new self.

Pain in My Head

Maniac: maniacal depression, a dynamic mixture of
pain and joy,
A wine of deception, a poison that runs deep.
My suffering makes me drunk with an unspeakable
pain.
Relief only comes through wild imaginings of
impossibilities.
My mind and body are spent, with a Hellish
hopelessness.
I struggle in vain to contain it, but I'm a broken wine
bottle.

Hopeless Life

I live an empty existence.
I am hopeless; life is that empty bottle of pain.
I don't want life in this dreamy darkness.
This callous world swallows me deeper.

People wound me with malicious lies; I'm filled with
the vinegar of falsity.
I thirst to fill my desert-parched existence.
Sad, all I see in this earthly grandeur is a polluted
oasis of deception.
Life is its own desolation.

I hate this world with such passionate intensity.
My mind is a Roman ruin.
My hands writhe with leprosy.
I cannot cure this cancerous plague that has befallen
me.

I live a cold, empty existence.
Life isn't worth the time it occupies.
I pray to the Lord, but He ignores me with laughter.
I fear that my only relief is an alcoholic decay.

Business Deal

Life, a grand marketplace of deceit and malice:
The Soul's fruit ripens with evil as man matures in
deception.
A soul's currency pays for this pleasant fiction.
With coins of the soul, we purchase acceptance and
friendship.
We shake hands with the devil only to be left in a
quiet despair.

Dark Karma

A black portentous cloud of hellish thoughts and
emotions, brewing like a storm,
Rains down heavy and rigid hail on the mirror of my
consciousness.
My face, writhing with agony and despair, reflects in
the little broken pieces of Old.
For now, I sense the deception and malice that has
eluded me for all this time.
The artifice's veil has been lifted; the truth can no
longer hide from its Dark Prince.
The bridge of my being, my psyche, is stimulated to
a chaotic expression.
His only anecdote for his wicked ailments is his
meditative endeavors toward the holy ideals.

Destiny of a Lost Soul

The grand Roman ruins of my mind are an empire of great evil and even greater despair and turmoil. The artful and decadent walls of corruption have met their ultimate fate and have fallen. The deceptive strength of the pillars of arrogance, ignorance, hate, anger, dishonesty, and dishonorable conduct have fallen under the weight of their own falsity. The artificial grandeur of my mind is no more; the decay within has now become the Hellish face of a dead era. All my royal, demonic powers and gifts have left me. Demonic gods, my great and cruel manipulators, no longer pretend to be my sycophants. The foundation of lies has now corroded under my feet, only to become a sharp and rigid quicksand, swallowing me alive; my own doing has now become my demise. However, all is not lost—a celestial hand, the hand of the Heavenly Father, reaches out to help me. He grabs my filthy hand and pulls me out of my ill-fated destiny. He shines his holy and restorative luminosity on my decaying spirit and places a seed of salvation in my heart. In my ear, the Almighty whispers, "Work out your own salvation with fear and trembling."

God in Every Life

Every breath, every life: six billion beating hearts;
the sound of one heartbeat to the melodious
attunement of God's spirit.

The ebb and flow of existence, the bloom of the
morning iris, and chariots of a nuclear fire usher in a
new light of consciousness.

The eclipse of the sun whispers the very secrets of
flesh and blood by the radiation of a solar tale.

The forgiving rains of a majestic earth give birth to
new bodies of cleansing grace.

I have now experienced the ecstasy of a newborn
child. Under the protective shadows of the oak tree, I
am free from worry.

The secrets of the foundation of the world, the reality
of consciousness: God brings life in every breath and
to every soul.

Restored Personality

The geometric walls of personality emanate a soul's mirror reflection; the mirrors no longer reflect my soul's expression, broken from the Hellish disarray and despair of the world. The crystal clear, reflective walls no longer stand in their mighty grandeur. They have met a broken, ill fate, shattering into a temporary waterfall of little, shimmering crystals—a sign of the dying era. However, from the untimely forfeit of a mighty infrastructure stems an even mightier creative force. A holy intercession from the hands of an imperial carpenter; the gracious hands of the heavenly father descend and create in me a new, vibrant city of imperishable crystal. I am restored and made whole with personality not of man, but of the Almighty.

Vanessa Hertweck: God's Eternal Rose

You are a gift from the Eternal God, a bright red rose adorned with dark purple leaves and a sleeve of dark green at the purple's edge; your beauty is striking, as fierce as a white tiger.

The Breath of God ushers in and engulfs you like a powerful hurricane. His Breath, His Spirit, His Love for you ignites the air into a softly roaring fire. You burn without burning and become one with the fire.

Your beauty is like a million brightly blue sapphire rubies in the Hand of God, being poured like a waterfall from the highest mountain. Your blue radiance is as breathtaking as an orgasm of heaven, echoing throughout the earth; it brings my soul to the climax of revelation.

My spirit ejaculates from my body, and I step into the garden of Eden. Rich is your vegetation! Your warm scent is succulent to my nostrils! Your sensual female scent roller-coasts my senses to the headiness of a mad ape and makes my heart roar like an African lion.

Your soil is soft and rich with life; it is firm

underneath my toes and invigorates my legs to ecstasy. You make it hard to stand, but my faith in God is my strength.

I walk a little further; I see you burning with beauty. Your sparkle is that of a ruby. Your soul is more precious than gold and silver.

The closer I get to you, the more intoxicated by your beauty I become. It is as fiery, purplish, dark green marijuana smoke in my lungs and a fine wine in my heart. My mind is doing cycles, riding on a sweet stream of ecstasy.

I go too high, but God grounds me in His wisdom. Your fiery smoke emanates from your rose, and it sets my mind ablaze. When I saw you in the flesh, the earth shook and stars illuminated the sky.

How lovely you are, my sexy little rose! Your hair falls straight and ends curly along your supple skin and shoulders. Your peachy, fair skin is like the serene blanket of winter snow, defying the softly roaring fire around you.

Your Chastity is protected. You are a virgin princess, with the ruby eyes of an African Queen. Rose petals adorn your small, firm breasts, and that sugary sweet spot between your legs is hidden by the rose petals of Life.

Your kisses give birth to a thousand rose petals, and your lips are as choice fruits. Your fruit juices are as mature as fine wine, and the aftertaste of your lips are like milk chocolate.

Your personality drips honey and milk, and your sexy mannerisms are coconut cream in my mouth. You are so good that you are evil. A tasty devil, you dominate my mind.

Your breasts are two shots of Vodka, and your sugary cunt is cocaine in my nostrils; even your petite ass is like a basket of purple marijuana, with glistening hints of red hair. Should I hate you or should I love you? God, deliver me from this sexy confusion! Yet, I still want more of your poison. Bite me like a Queen Cobra, trap me in your web like a Black Widow spider, devour me like an African Lioness, and consume me in your nature!

My Mind becomes crazed with thoughts of you. My heart fights to discern your mysteries. In my infatuation with you, I want to strangle you, squeezing your throat to a lifeless end. No! I want to hold you, softly feeling your warmth for eternity.

God slaps me out of my insanity, and I find peace in Him. I enjoy you from the distance of God. You are not my rose, but the rose of God! I return back to my body, wiser than when I left it.

Defining My Existence

Rigorous and meditative endeavors decipher the duality of existence:

I have already broken the complexity of the law of attraction and repulsion in my simplicity.

I seek to find that which I have lost.

I seek to find the wonderful face of the Heavenly Father.

I seek, so I shall find imperishable life.

Holy Pathway

My mental disposition has given birth to a long, frightful, evil dream. Like a dark karmic cloud, demonic vultures have locked the very radiance of God's light in the virginal aspect of my psyche. I am left in a state of decaying and lifeless movement; growing weaker and weaker, I painfully moan to the Lord, "Please have mercy, I have been a fool! Make a way for me out of this Hellish desolation!" The Lord sends his mighty celestial servant, Archangel Michael, who wields his imperial flaming sword with such grandeur, striking through the dark clouds of sin with a magnificent thunderbolt of fire. The once insipid and death-stricken air is now ionized with righteous and cleansing, electric fire, giving way to heaven's spiritual luminosity. The light nourishes my soul and illuminates the unconsciousness within me. I am revived and endowed with newfound strength; the unconsciousness becomes aware of itself. With a small gesture of his flaming sword, he opens a pathway to imperishable salvation. Celestial words are engraved into the paved, stone pathway: Wisdom, Temperance, Fortitude, and Justice. My conscious being walks the long path from its dualistic awareness to its true source: the Heavenly Father.

Contemplation of the Truth

I look back at the clear, watery reflection of my
memories.
I finally see life without the distortion of perception.
I witness a man deeply gazing back at me, his eyes
like an inferno.
I see myself, and finally, I understand that I'm to
blame for my despair.
As I gaze at the Omni-truth in the eyes, the destiny
of my soul is revealed.
I am engulfed in the quickening fire of the Almighty
Truth.
I scream, but I am unable to flee. I am paralyzed in
my own reality.

School of Fire

I failed to listen to the portentous warnings of wisdom. She warned me of the malicious ways of the world, but I would not hear her truth. However, because of her ceaseless love, she gave me over to my most pure of enemies: my friends, my harsh brothers and sisters. Through their glassy eyes, I saw my many weaknesses. Their cruel and tormenting insults taught me how to find inner strength. They burned my flesh with their disdainful eyes, only to leave me in a cold and bitter isolation. I thirsted for acceptance, but to no avail. I craved true friendship, but none would have me, since I lived like a sinful fool. I was like a man with leprosy. Like the ancient blacksmith, God used my peers to help me realize and beat out the impurities of my fleeting life. With eyes wide open, I saw myself as I saw the world. Like me, the world was filled with rancor and deceit. The poison that resided in my soul permeated to my outward being; I became blind and knew not why I stumbled. When I rose to my feet, I finally understood the great love of wisdom. God used my enemies to make me stronger; it was my enemies who crushed me, and by God's hand, it was my enemies who helped rebuild me…God bless my most cruel and enriching teachers.

Noumenon[5]

Thought and mind are separate in locality but one in self-expression. Fire of thought, the warm radiance of the cosmic intelligence, fills the empty abyss of my mind:

I am alive.

I am full.

I am quiet.

I am a poetic philosopher.

I'm aware of the Great Knowledge that I know absolutely nothing.

---

[5] Noumenon – In the philosophy of Kant, an object as it is in itself, independent of the mind; as opposed to a phenomenon.

Pregnant with Destiny

A marital sage finds stillness in his mental palace of chaotic intelligence: the serene structure born from the perpetually modulating, the geometric atmosphere of divine, unique, and artful creativity. In the vague walls of transparent thickness, he is quickened with a cumulative spiritual and mundane awareness of his true self, a gracious endowment from the imperial Sensei Jesus. This celestial gift of sharp purpose is his metaphorical sword: a pen of divine gold and silver to reflect God's astronomical light of glory. His mind and body are not of his own, pregnant with this arduous task to save himself and the decadent world.

Ernest Antwi

Path to Kinghood

Lord God, to you all the Praise and Glory!

My earthly family has left my mouth as a parched desert, not an oasis of relief in sight.

My friends have become an arm of dry and chapped flesh.

Even the people I see daily are as painful as sores on my head.

I look around me and find no help in sight; I am alone and lost in this void that screams nothingness.

In my trial and anguish, I find that You, not man, are my only comfort in this testing.

Your Word is food to my soul. My thoughts become the knowledge of Your Word, and my heart is a strong river, reflecting the light of Your Holy Spirit.

In You and by Your Word, I step into a wealthy place. The oasis of my mouth is resolved, and my tongue flows with life.

My arms are no longer tormented; instead they are strong in the dew of Your presence and rejuvenation.

Your knowledge has become wisdom in my heart, and I now discipline my foes to Your Word.

The Mighty Lord God enthroned in Heaven has crafted a crown for my head. I have gone through my trial of fire and water. You have proven me by the torments of my enemies.

You have anointed me King in the midst of my enemies; Your wisdom is perfect!

Ernest Antwi